Mr Sagittarius

Poetry & Prose

M J MALLON

KYROSMAGICA PUBLISHING

Mr. Sagittarius Poetry and Prose
© 2020 M J Mallon

A legal deposit record for this book is to be held at the British Library, National Library of Scotland, The Bodleian Library Oxford University, National Library of Wales, Cambridge University Library, and the Library of Trinity College Dublin.

Paperback ISBN: 978-1-9998224-4-6

Published in Kindle and paperback February 2020

Kyrosmagica Publishing
mjmallon.com

Cover Design by Rachael Ritchey: https://rachaelritchey.com/
Photography: All photography by the author, except two photos donated by Alex Marlowe via Samantha Murdoch.

Dedication

Dedicated to the wondrous splendour of the natural world, to the trees, flowers and magical creatures which grace our gardens, meadows, open spaces and forests. Inspired by the magnificent botanical gardens around the world, my personal favourites being: Cambridge, Edinburgh, and Montreal.

Table of Contents

The Golden Weeping Willow

William walked through the snow-laden bamboo archway towards the icy water. He knew where he was going and that thought alone brought an enormous lump to his throat. The lump grew into a bulb that threatened to burst. He willed it down, he couldn't cry, not here in public.

The bench was situated where he and his brother Harold had often sat under the golden weeping willow tree, right by the water's edge. The branches and leaves of the tree created a lengthy curtain which twinkled with filaments of spell-binding snow.

Inscribed on the bench were the words:

For Harold, who loved the garden's seasons, the rainbows, and the distant twinkling lights. The trees, the birds, and flowers and most of all the beautiful dragonflies who bring an aura of magic with their short lives.

Dragonfly
Red, devil's needle,
Or luck bringer with kind eyes?
Ancient, sweet fellow,
Sacred magic bestower,
Change tumbling on fragile wings.

William sat down on the bench, the lump in his throat burst and a dam of tears flowed from the well of his soul. The weeping willow tree bent its snow encrusted branches towards him, and little jewels of snow fell upon him. He glanced to his left and saw a dragonfly sitting next to him. How extraordinary to see a dragonfly in winter! He remembered he'd seen a dragonfly the last time that Harold had been here with him. It had hovered above a kahili ginger lily. The weather had been sunny that day.

Today's dragonfly was red with two black dots on its tail. Its crystalline wings were delicate, and each had brown frosty markings highlighting it. The dragonfly didn't move, so William put his hand just above it. It didn't flutter away. It stayed motionless, as if the freezing temperatures were exhausting the creature. William put his hand next to it and again the dragonfly remained.

William was alone, so he chatted to the dragonfly. It wasn't something he would normally do, but this wasn't a normal day. He had heard that dragonflies were lucky, and some people even believed they denoted the potential for change. Surely that had to be promising?

"Hi, Mr. dragonfly," he whispered. "I guess you're a Mr.? It's good to see you. I'm glad you're here. It gets cold in winter for us old ones, don't feel bad for resting a while."

The dragonfly lifted off the bench for a second and landed near William's shoulder. It stared at him with its perceptive eyes as if it was listening.

"I'm glad to see you're not too worn out, or frozen to fly. You, and your insect friends the butterflies have such a short but sweet life. Ah, life is too short. I miss my twin brother Harold so much. It's like I've lost myself and I can't get back to being me without him by my side."

The dragonfly flew up and floated above William's head and whizzed about as if trying to say something.

William knew what the dragonfly meant. It didn't have to speak, William just knew. It was like they were two ancient creatures sharing a silent chinwag.

He got up slowly, as his poor old limbs had forgotten how to get up fast. He had to buy something, or make something, that would connect him to Harold. The dragonfly's momentary visit gave him the wisdom to understand this.

When William walked into his flat, he nearly had a heart attack. It didn't look like his flat anymore. There were female touches everywhere, and the aroma was orange-clove mixed with pine, the overall effect clean, and tidy.

"Annette, what in the blazes!" he yelled. "Is this even my home?" he cried.

"Ungrateful so and so," exclaimed Annette. She was clutching a broom and looked in grave danger of whacking him with it.

"It's my flat and you've turned it into a… a smelly tart's boudoir," cried William.

Annette lifted the broom, walked towards him and poked the broom under his nose.

"I've had enough," she exclaimed. "After Harold's death I came here to clean, cook and care for you and now this. You, ungrateful devil! I've had enough. Christmas, or no Christmas I'm going."

She let go of the broom; it clattered to the floor with a crashing sound.

With her nose in the air, she picked up her jacket from the coat stand. Making a show of her escalating anger she stamped her feet as she walked towards the door.

William moved as fast as his old legs could take him. He got to the door just in time to barricade her exit.

"I'm sorry Annette. I shouldn't have said what I did, grief makes people say things they shouldn't," he said trembling.

"Grief! That wasn't grief speaking, you idiot. That was you, being you! You're grieving but I am too. He was my brother too. You've always hogged him. Twins. Brothers! What about me, I'm your only sister!"

"I had no idea Annette," William scratched his head. "I know you're my only sister, but I had no clue you felt so left out."

"Huh. Everyone knew, except you and your precious Harold. Both of you are... he was, you are, visually and emotionally impaired!"

"I'm sorry. I'll make it up to you, I promise."

Annette bent down to pick up the broom. She paused for a moment as if she was considering what to do next. William stepped back a bit and nearly tripped. She sighed and put the broom away.

They walked towards each other. Each step taking them to that point when they were asking a silent question. Then they hugged for a long time. It was the first hug they'd shared in ages.

"Sis, I'll make you a lovely cup of tea," said William as he gently moved away from the hug and walked towards the kettle. "Sit down, I'll fetch you some biscuits too."

Annette's face screwed up in puzzlement. "Biscuits?"

"Yes, I got some in town."

"But you never eat biscuits. That was always Harold's..."

"I know but I thought it might bring us closer together if I shared some things he liked to do, other than being impulsive and chasing women!"

"Oh," she replied, her eyes wide with recollection. She paused for a moment remembering. "Yes, he had many lady friends did our Harold. Remember that memorial request he made? It was a shame we found it too late. Referring to his lovers as if they were flowers and calling himself Mr. Sagittarius!"

"Yes, he could be very odd, could Harold. But, very entertaining too! Do you think we did the right thing Annette? Do you think we should have changed the plaque after discovering his request?"

Annette paused for a moment considering. "No, we did the right thing William."

"Yes, maybe I'm over thinking it."

Annette remained silent for a long while but when she spoke her eyes brightened. "So where are these fabulous biscuits and fine tea?"

"Here."

"I see," replied Annette, with a disappointed look on her face.

The biscuits were plain, the type you dunk in tea and get soggy.

William's face fell.

"Oh, stop pulling such a face William. This might be fun. Why not? Let's dunk," said Annette, making light of it.

They drank their tea and dunked their biscuits and Annette knitted. She had a big bag of wool to make a rainbow hat for William. The rainbow hat that Harold would have loved for a Christmas gift.

With the colours of the rainbow and the dragonfly's colours: red, brown, black and shimmering silver and the lightest of fingers to create it. It had to be just right, so it could fly off William's head like a dragonfly light and quick. If it fitted too tight, or too close to the scalp it would be useless.

Throughout the night they consumed copious amounts of tea and biscuit barrels of biscuits. Annette knitted until her hands ached. Luckily, she had no arthritis, her hands were still nimble. At last the hat was ready.

"Try it on," prompted Annette.

William popped it on his head and Annette smiled. It was perfect, not too tight, not too loose.

"It couldn't be better. Look at you! Harold must be smiling down on us. We'll go to the botanical gardens tomorrow." suggested Annette. "But for now, I'm tired, so I'm off to bed."

"Yes, tomorrow we'll visit Harold's bench by the weeping willow tree. The hat is amazing, and you are too. Sorry for being such a rubbish big brother."

Annette smiled, she got up slowly and put her knitting bag away. She turned to look at William wearing the rainbow hat before she made her way up the stairs to bed.

William sat for a while in quiet contemplation before he eased his tired limbs up to navigate the stairs to his bedroom.

First things first, he brushed his teeth and put his pyjamas on. He left the hat on his head. He feared that if he took it off, perhaps he might not live to see another day, or he might not find it again. The hat felt too light, too adventurous, and too mischievous not to keep it by him always.

Miraculously, the next day the hat was still clinging to the tip of his head when he woke up. He breathed a sigh of relief.

He joined Annette to have a quick breakfast of tea, and cereal. Then they headed off to the botanical gardens. The lady on the welcome desk greeted them with a big smile.

"Ah, you've brought your sister. How nice. I'm so very sorry to hear about Harold. How are you bearing up Annette?"

"It's been a sad time. I came to give William a helping hand. I'm bone tired, my crazy brother kept me up all night knitting."

"Oh," replied the woman looking somewhat perplexed. "What did you knit?"

William pointed at the hat on his head. The lady squinted.

"Oh, I see it now. The winter sun was shining so much I couldn't see your hat. Wow, that's some hat. It's like a rainbow's resting perched on your head. That's so special, you better not lose it, William! It must have taken ages for your sister to make for you."

Annette smiled. It had taken her one night, no more no less.

They went to Harold's bench by the weeping willow tree and sat and waited. They knew what they wanted, and they knew what they hoped for. For, a long time they waited in vain. No

Harold. Then, William stood up and looked at his reflection in the water beside the weeping willow tree.

Suddenly his reflection changed. He saw Harold wearing the hat at a jaunty angle.

"Look Annette," William said pointing. "I can see Harold wearing the hat."

As Annette looked, a tiny tear escaped from her eyes. "It's you William. Just you."

William sighed. He saw some winter frosted flowers by the water's edge. The magical dragonfly rested by them. William tried to bend down, to kneel before it but he only got so far when his knees locked. So, in desperation he pleaded. "Tell me what to do, mighty dragonfly. I'm stuck!"

The dragonfly didn't speak. Dragonflies don't, but a whisper in the breeze carried a sound that echoed in William's ears.

It said one word: "believe."

William unlocked his knees. He felt the hat moving on his head; it lifted off with a sudden gust of wind and flew up and away. He tried to run after it, but he could no longer run, his aging limbs moved but they were slow. The hat danced and rolled, gyrating with a burst of energy until it landed on top of a tree branch well beyond his reach.

Next to it William spotted a ginger tom cat he had never seen before. Where had it appeared from? The cat grinned. It curled up in the tree next to the hat as if settling in for a nightcap.

The hat created a brilliant snatch of colour on the tree next to the ginger-coloured tom cat.

⚜

A rumour abounds that every Christmas the magical cat and the hat move from branch to branch with the spellbinding dragonfly when nobody's looking. If you can see them, you are in tune with the Christmas spirit of the golden weeping willow tree.

Stay a while and rest your weary limbs. See whose reflection you may see in the pond. The magic of Christmas past, future and present survives within the water's essence but only those ancient enough to believe will delight in knowing.

Golden Willow Tree

So charming you are
Sweet golden willow bending
Longing for water
Not I, deep depths frighten me
I long to touch you… alas…
Pleasing temptation

Your branches beckon nearer
No danger greater
I dangle closer
To make an uncomely splash.

Robin: Etheree

Bench,
A bird,
Red-breasted,
So, tame you rest,
Beside me robin,
Two friends on a park bench,
One human, one of nature,
I appreciate your kind time,
Until you away… exploring far,
Hinting at possibilities you go.
I wonder what you notice in your world.
And why you choose that ground to explore,
When you could have stayed here with me,
In mindful meditation.
Maybe you'll visit me,
Christmas day, perhaps?
To bring good cheer,
Until then,
Peace to,
You.

Life Lessons from Buddha

Buddha teaches us
To develop good habits
Time to meditate
Ensconced by a sacred tree
While sweet birds serenade you.

Life Lessons from Cats

Image of cat via Alex Marlowe.

Bound about, stay curious,
Extol trying hard,
Do what's right for you, RELAX....
Live, love, unconditionally.
Be determined but have FUN.

Mr. Frowning Tree

An expressive face
Full of such feeling
Carved in wood. I pause.

Mr. Frowning Tree,
Stops me on my way to work,
With his cheeky frown,
Little devil what a tease,
I doubt he's really that sad!

Rainbow Child

Young Aurora collected rainbows like other children collect shells and pretty trinkets. She learnt all there was to know about these wonders of reflection and refraction but longed to see a very special sight–a double rainbow with a second arc visible outside the primary arc. She'd heard an ancient legend that the only way to call such a rainbow forth would be to carry tourmaline on her, so she sought out a beautiful necklace with the finest tourmaline crystal embedded in its pendant.

Image of Tourmaline via Alex Marlowe.

As soon as she placed the tourmaline around her neck, she felt an extraordinary sensation of blood pumping in her veins. It was so loud that she covered her ears with her hands and screwed her eyes tight. After a while, her nervous system settled, the pounding subsided, and she removed her hands. She heard an ancient voice speaking to her coming from the centre of the stone. The voice held a special quality in its tone. Each syllable it spoke conjured up many vibrant colours in her mind.

"Young Aurora. This tourmaline is yours now; it shines for you, rainbow child. It is a very special crystal found in all imaginable colours. It is the only crystal to have travelled along a rainbow and as it did, it collected the entire rainbow's colours."

Aurora smiled. The words reassured her; she sensed that the tourmaline would bring her face-to-face with her much desired double rainbow.

The next day, she stepped out into the garden. The air felt fresh and moist as it had been raining. The rain continued to fall carrying tiny little rainbow splashes of joy which landed leaving behind a multitude of colour and a twinkling sound. As the rain fell on her clothes, each item of her clothing turned bright and magnificent reflecting all the colours of the rainbow and many more besides: red, orange, yellow, green, blue, indigo and violet. She looked up and saw the most magnificent double rainbow in the sky. Her hand went to her lips as she gasped in surprise. The tourmaline hummed a tune rich with happiness and exaltation.

Aurora skipped in the garden, treading on the rainbow puddles that lay forming a pathway. Each puddle grew more brilliant as she hopscotched further ahead. At the end of the puddles she came across a table and chair, she had never seen before. A rainbow parasol shielded the table, and a pristine white sheet of paper and a pen lay waiting for her untouched.

She sat down, picked up the pen, and heard the ancient voice again.

"Aurora, you have found your double rainbow. Now write, child. Tourmaline will inspire your creativity. Today, write from your heart about your magnificent rainbow."

Aurora's eyes gleamed with excitement. She didn't hesitate; she pressed the nib of the pen to the paper, but no words came, not one. She frowned and tried again. But the pen drew no words forth. She knelt to the ground, dipped the nib of the pen in a puddle of a rainbow and pressed the anointed nib to the paper. At last the words flowed in a myriad of colours filling the white page with a colourful rainbow of verse.

Dear rainbow, so fine,
Your colours reversed,
Red on your inner side arc,
Double beauty, discovered.
Never leave me, dearest heart.
Parasol of light,
Rainbow of colours divine,
Warming my soul,
Sweet route to inspiration,
Hide me from pain and suffering.
Red, and yellow, blue,
Indigo and violet,
Many coloured dreams,
Such a beauty, shining joy,
Create with me, my rainbow friends.

She placed the pen down and felt an extraordinary lightness of spirit. She danced and danced, her skirt swirling around, unravelling and widening in an arc of spectacular colours as she moved. Soon, she had a curious crowd of onlookers. The shy hedgehog came out of his hiding place, followed by the birds, cats, butterflies, and even the reticent worms poked their heads out of the ground to join in with her happiness.

Such is the power of a double rainbow; it warms our hearts after the sky pours down its sadness in raindrops. We become refreshed and renewed, ready and willing to embrace new friends. Our new found friends will be our best friends, our rainbow friends, who will support us through dark times and the sunshine.

Friends for Tea

Whose blue bike is that?
Oh wait, I see your shadow
Two bikes and two chairs
Two fruit scones, butter and jam
Two old friends sit by the light

After the twin's funeral Annette arrives back home to an empty house. She opens the fridge door and finds nothing, not a loaf of bread, or a mouse on the countertop to befriend her. Disheartened, she sits down by the bare kitchen table, exhausted. It has been so hard to bear; both her twin brothers dying so soon after each other. How cruel. Tears threaten to escape her eyes, but she wipes them away, chiding herself for being weak. She contemplates buying some groceries but the thought of that just exhausts her more. Her eyes begin to feel heavy, soon she is dreaming of a time when the three of them were young and life was full of excitement especially at Halloween.

The Candy Corn Monster

The Candy corn Monster,
Lives alone.
They say he gobbles candy.

They say he doesn't share.
They say his tummy's big,
But his yellow, orange and white eyes are bigger.

His house lies in shadows,
But I'm not scared.

I'll knock on his door with a rat, tat, tat.
He'll growl, and growl,
Until I give him a gigantic kiss!

I'll shine a beam of light in his eyes!
He'll drop all his candy quick,
I'll grab it fast!

See Candy corn is for sharing,
No ifs, no buts, he must see,
We're all little monsters, him and me!

Candyfloss Critter

Glowing in the night,
A sugar bonbon tease,
Candyfloss critter,
Tennis ball,
Lying in the grass.

Hidden amongst gravestones,
It implores - Pick me up,
Roll me, throw me, catch me!
Join the dead who come to play,
Cemetery games.

Wicked trees carve possibilities,
Gnarled branches twist,
Hush, whisper,
Freeze frame this moment,
Temptation on a knife edge.

I resist!
An ancient ball gleams anew,
Rainbows of magical colours entice,
I weaken - It candy pops,
An imaginary snack in my hand.

I stagger, fall back,
Words whizzing, powerful,
First serves, my opponent,
Wins, Game Set and Match,
This is no Facebook funny - Simon's Cat.

Instead a demon Cheshire cat,
With sharpened fangs,
Devours my imagination,
Savouring me, the delicacy,
It grins, its tummy full of my thoughts.

It licks its greedy lips,
Sits in the tree,
Hoping a writer will pass by soon,
Too curious to walk away,
Another Halloween victim.

Looking back in time, Annette remembers a tragedy. After which, Halloween lost its sparkle for a time and today that feeling of loss persists. The sights and sounds of that tragic time flicker like a technicolour reel in Annette's mind, tormenting her in quiet moments.

Mr Ghost With Ease

I've always been a joker,
But now the joke's on me,
Death made a fool of me,
Tra la la, come along you'll see.

I chose to bike to school,
Each and every day,
Didn't see it coming,
'cause I needed a wee.

My jokes were flattened,
Wheels crushed me on my bike,
Life wiped in an instant,
No more tee hee, hee.

So, nothing to do,
But play this game instead,
Every wicked Halloween I follow,
So, you'll remember me.

I don't need no costume,
No vampire cape, no broom,
I leave the wizards' breathless
With my deadliest sneeze,

I'm a ghost with ease, mingling,
With the laughing living,

A cheeky treat or trick am I,
A giggling ghost who likes to please,
There's one girl who sees me,
She doesn't tell a soul,
No one would likely listen,
To her pleading pleas,

I like her. You would too,
I need a friend who's different,
But sort of same as me,
Kind of a touchy, tearaway tease,

She's a witch dressed in black,
Who brings a creepy cat,
Doesn't own it, doesn't matter,
Except for them fierce-some fleas.

'Purr,' says the cat, 'I'm brutal black,'
Like boy's heart too,
Used to be a deep, rich red,
Sturdy planted like the trees.

'Good,' says the boy, 'I want to be,'
But death has made me bad,
I am jealous, angry, wicked,
From here to where I have no knees.

Which witch will live this Halloween?
Vampire. Cross the road, survive,
Demon. No one knows but me,
Wizard. Kills, lives, you will see!

Annette is now getting old. She continues to thrive with few ailments, and her quick mind endures many calamities. A quiet acceptance has settled upon her calming her once voluminous temper. But her dreams refuse to stay quiet, they frighten her with their contrary, and often confusing messages.

Dreaming at Halloween

I dream in colour,
But now everything is dark,
Where has the light gone?
Oh, cruel leafy canopy,
No green meadow, just blue thoughts.

A spectre haunts me,
Through the trees he drifts slowly,
I hear no weeping,
Just a tall, grey wall of sighs,
Twigs snap, and nothing changes.

Annette's twin brothers Harold and William plaque has become weathered and almost impossible to read. Mysteries about them abound. Neither of them had ever married.

Ode to Love - Eternal

Love is ethereal
A spark of brilliance
Brimming with possibilities
Delicate, it survives

We long to believe
Its eternal truth
Like a spectre
We seek its beauty
Once awaken it never dies.

William's love life had proved to be an enigma to Annette. She was at a loss to know if he ever loved, or if he was happy to live alone.

Love Taken By Death: Diamante

Love
Passionate, Amorous
Rousing, Stimulating, Inciting
Emotion, Feelings, Anger, Regret,
Longing, Craving, Desiring,
Stirring, Blinding,
Yearning, Despair.

Ghost: Septolet

Ghost
Denied kisses
Once cherished

———

Ghost pleads waiting
For a kiss
Forsaken
By Death

A Face on Bark: Etheree

I
See you
In the trees
A face on bark
Your sad love me look
The way nature moved you
My champion, darling,
Giant man, never forgotten,
Colossal reach beyond desire.
A network of roots bring me to your heart.

The seasons come and go, and life's circle continues… a blur of memorable colour, sunshine, raindrops, earnestness and ridiculousness.

Lollipop Sunshine Tree

Lollipop yellow
Leaves fall in fragile raindrops
Winter thoughts arrive.
Sweet autumn dissolving fast
Leaving sunshine memories

For Mr. Snowman

This snowman's vigour,
Frosty spirit caught my eye,
He winked, the snow fell,
Such a smile melted my heart,
Sweet guy stay a-while!

Annette's thoughts return to a delightful Christmas long ago. Her then husband had filled her stocking full of delightful treats. A tiny bubble bath hidden at the bottom of her stocking, nearly escapes her attention. It's labelled with the words: Serena's Bubble Magic. When Annette opens the lid, she breathes in such an enchanting, intoxicating scent that she pours the whole contents into her bath that very night. The bottle is small, but the bubbles keep on coming and coming; she wonders if they will ever stop!

Serena's Christmas Bubble Monster

Serena turned the tap on full blast. The candles flickered creating a relaxing ambience. She poured herself a large glass of wine and gulped it down in one big glug. Then she poured another. Continuing in the same vein she tipped the whole bottle of her favourite scented apple bubble bath in. No half measures. Not tonight. The bubbles grew and grew until they resembled a very large foamy marshmallow; the aroma reminding her of the imagined scent of a delightful apple orchard.

Serena was hungry and the apple scent would have tempted her to eat this apple marshmallow feast if she wasn't certain that it was a bubble bath. The white bubbly marshmallow spread out in a most peculiar way, whipping around like an enormous candy floss generator growing bigger and bigger. Boy, her low blood sugar level was getting to her! Serena tried to turn the tap off, but it was stuck. The water just kept on coming, gushing out faster and faster. Serena dashed around the bathroom, desperately looking for something to grip the tap with. In the process the towel she had secured around her body nearly fell off. She found a hand towel and tried turning the tap off again. Still no luck. If the water wouldn't stop, it would flood the house, and this foaming marshmallow bubble would keep on growing and growing.

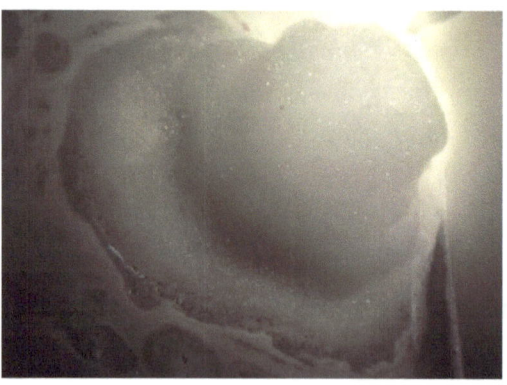

Serena sensed this was beyond the scope of her normal realm of experience. She couldn't google this. In desperation she shouted for her husband, but he didn't come. He must have fallen asleep in front of the TV, been listening to loud music, or gone to the pub without telling her. That sounded more likely. Ugh. Men!

She shouted again, and this time, she got a reply, a response she wasn't expecting.

"Stop shouting! Can't you see I've got an important job on. You're agitating me, and agitated bubbles make for an agitated fellow, and I'm sure you wouldn't want that!"

The bubbles could talk? How peculiar! They sounded like a gush of water you might hear at the end of a very long ride at your favourite water park.

This fountain of exploding bubbles waved its soapy arms about in distress, sending little clouds of foam tumbling in all directions.

Serena gasped. The bubbles were frothing and foaming and getting more distinct by the minute. The bubble creature was now the size of a little man, who appeared to be frowning.

"Oh, stop it! Will you stop it! Just for a minute, please, Mr. what can I call you?" shouted Serena.

"I'm forgetting my manners, do accept my apologies, my dear. I'm... Mr. Bubble Monster," he replied with a soapy frown.

This was the last straw, Serena found herself on the verge of tears. It had been a stressful week; she had run up a huge phone bill, been involved in a minor accident, and had a row with her husband.

"Stop creeping me out, Mr. Bubble whatever you are," she cried.

"Creeping you out, heavens to soap suds, I'm just teasing! Come now, can't you take a joke? How could a Bubble Monster be creeping you out? I'm just made from hot steamy water, and friendly bubbles!"

Serena saw her mistake, really it had been an overly stressful week. "Now that I look at you more closely, I don't think you look frightening, but I'm not sure what you are. You're flicking bubbles everywhere, and if you keep this up, you'll flood my house."

"I don't flood houses, well not often, only when I'm very cross. Today I'm in a good mood. I loved your apple bubble bath, what a lovely smell, so fresh and inviting. Lovely candles too, just what the doctor ordered, Serena, you have a great taste in bubble bath. I love your name, Serena, very Serene. It's just about good enough to eat, oh, not you, my dear, your bubble bath. I feel like a new, improved Bubble Monster now. I needed that so much, and lots of hot water, it's so important, you'll see, just one second," the bubble monster reached over with his foamy hand and turned the tap.

The tap groaned and shrieked as if it was in terrible pain and then the water stopped.

"How did you do that?" asked Serena, her forehead creasing with confusion.

"Bubble magic. Next time you run a bubble bath, remember my motto: Bubbles are magic, and magic must never ever be wasted."

"Oh, now I see, you're cross with me for emptying the whole of the bubble bath in."

"Of course, I am, well said," said the bubble monster as he started to dissolve, his foamy body disappearing one bubble at a time down the plughole.

"Hey, don't go," said Serena, dashing forward as if she was about to catch him.

"Sorry I've got to rush. Shame really. Tut Tut, my soapy radar tells me someone else is up to bubble mischief."

The Bubble Monster shook his soapy head, sending specks of bubbles everywhere.

The Bubble Monster began to shrink in size. Soon there was nothing left of him but his neck, chin, and his head, all of which were resting right by the plug hole.

"We'll meet again, my dear," replied the Bubble Monster, his words barely audible, as parts of his head started to disappear.

"When?" asked Serena.

The Bubble Monster had to race to answer, his words speeding up, faster, and faster. "Soon. I'm sure of it. Buy more bubble bath. Light more candles. Atmosphere is everything. Don't use it all, but don't be stingggggy. I'll check. Take care, Serene Serena. Have a nice bath…YIKES…G O O D B Y EEEEEE…"

He managed one final lop-sided grin, and a mischievous bubbly wink, and then he disappeared.

Bubbly Snowman Kisses

The Bubble Monster,
Appears in all disguises,
Often, he may sing.

A hearty Snowman song,
On Snowy Christmas days,
He greets you.

Singing golden verses,
He's always chillingly sweet,
Jewelled admirer.

A Christmas cracker,
Bubbly terror of the tub,
So hot, he's soon gone!

Grab him while you can…
Watch out for his sweet kisses,
They might leave a mark.

Like all the cool guys,
He's bound to disappear,
Swirling down the plug.
Before he gets caught.

By much loved, bearded, guess who?
Prize bubble catcher.

Old Santa dear,
He'll get the reindeer on him,
Send him on his way.

Trying not to cry,
Tears drop into the hot tub,
I sigh, once, twice, thrice.

Farewell, Adieu,
Bubble monster - heart stealer,
Santa's cute rival!

By now Annette has lived alone for many years. She has only herself to converse with, her once busy household is a place of desperate whispers.

That Twinkle in Her Eyes is Magic

Buried,
Two dear husbands,
Five years ago they say,
Holding back tears threatening,
She sighs.
It weeps,
Her loneliness,
Pressing against breast bone,
Tender solar plexus aching,
Poor Dear.
Adjust

Her shoulder straps,
So they don't dig so much,
It's my job, but it's more than that.
Much more.
Offer
Her tea, coffee,
Water, no saccharin,
She only wants love, and lovers,
Listen.
Drinking,
Every word,
I gulp down her sweet life.
Thirst-quenching her lonely sorrow.
I see.
Her friend,
Met on a bus,
A random meeting place,
A common thread both are widows,
Both lost.
They found,
One another,
Instantly became friends,
A little lighter, the laughter,
Became.
Curtains,
New silhouette,
Her friend gasps, 'Beautiful.'
She says it and really means it.
I smile.
Sometimes,
Words wrap heartache,
In kind tender tissue,
To keep a safe, invincible.

Parcel.
Shining,
Her reflection,
Glows with vivaciousness,
Twinkle-eyed magic's desire,
Captured.
Husband,
Third time lucky,
He's on his way to her,
Doesn't know it yet but he is,
Old news.
Even,
If he's younger,
He'll not dare outlive her,
I see her living ninety plus.
Diva.
'Tis fact,
Not a figment,
Of some kind of fiction,
Clearly have it all figured out,
No chance.
I am,
Spellbound, lost,
In her new reflection,
The mirror glows with praise.
It basks.

Annette will meet her maker soon to await his judgment. Will he be kind, will he forgive her? Or will he find her lacking?

The Old Man of Snow and The Snow Snake

Today, the moon is full and high in the sky and a group of nineteen men travel with brave hearts to the mouth of the Snow Snake Cave.

The wind is biting cold. Each man carries a pack of provisions on his back and thoughts of his loved ones in his heart. They know that this journey might be one to their deaths and yet they trudge on.

At last after many exhausted steps they arrive at the forbidding entrance of the cave. It is no ordinary grotto. For centuries men have fashioned the cave out of layer upon layer of snow. The mouth of which is an ice sculpture of a snake's jaw gaping, its eyes furious and wide. The old man above is exquisite, his hair and snow beard fall in intricate icicles. He is leaning to one side, his hand of snow pushing down on the snake as if to coax it to move.

The Old Man of Snow startles the men, he stirs, his snow encrusted eyes open wide as he bellows,

"Dare you approach us? I think not little men. I will crush you like ants and feed you to my friend the Snow Snake."

The men stop so suddenly that they almost fall over with exhaustion. Several of them stagger backwards frightened by the sheer size and forbidding nature of the Old Man of Snow. But, one amongst them stays still, resolute and strong.

He squares his shoulders, takes a deep breath and replies. "I wish to meet with the Old Man of Snow and the legendary Snow Snake to discuss what you've done with the countless others who have ventured here. That is all that I and this brave group of men want—our old friends back. We are not greedy men. We don't desire wealth, or gold, we only want happiness."

"Happiness" the Old Man lifts his hand and pulls at his beard. The Snow Snake winds his tail back and forth causing a volley of tiny snowballs to fall.

"They are lying Old Man," said the Snow Snake, hissing. "They mean to trick us. Don't allow them passage. If you do, I will swish my furious tail even more and it will crush them under an avalanche of snow."

"Silence, Snow Snake! I am sick of your reptilian attitude. Let them speak. I have never heard a human ask for so little before and I am curious if they speak the truth."

The humble man bowed before the Old Man of Snow and then kneeled on the cold earth. "I swear by the almighty that I tell the truth. I, and my men are simple farmers, we tend the earth, eat our crops, and milk our herd. We don't need riches and fame."

"You are a wise man. Unfortunately, your friends who came before you were foolish and greedy. They tried to steal from the Snow Snake, and that made us very angry."

"They were wrong to do so and I apologise on their behalf. Please forgive me for asking but what happened to their foolish souls?"

"Within the cave there are a multitude of tiny snow snakes who wriggle free when they smell greed. These tiny snakes are lethal, one bite of their venom stilled these greedy men's hearts and froze them for all eternity. Here, come. I grant you entry to see the power we possess so you will not dare to steal from us. The ice sculptures of your friends are exquisite."

The men muttered. Some made as if to turn back but the leader spoke again.

"Men come with me, we must pay our respects to our old friends."

One replied, "Are you mad? They may do the same to us. How can you trust the Old Man of Snow, the Snow Snake and his allies the tiny venomous snakes?"

"I only know what is right and good," replied the humble man.

"So, will it be," said several of his followers, but many turned away, retracing their steps back from where they had come.

They granted the few that remained a passage into the mouth of the Snow Snake's cave. But the snake hissed and rattled his snow tail in a show of extreme displeasure.

The Old Man of snow stamped his snowy boots, and the snake stopped.

Once inside the cave, the humble man and his band of followers saw nothing but ice and snow. They heard no sign of life, no trickle of water, but still they walked on.

As they turned a corner, the cave widened, and they entered a room which was ablaze with a colourful array of magical stones. For a moment it tempted even the humble man to pop one of these magnificent stones in his pocket but then he remembered the Old Man's warning.

The men began to question their desires. "Surely one small stone for each of us wouldn't be a wicked thing to do?" they clamoured.

The humble man turned to them and spoke. "We are here to save our friends, not to steal. We must save them or bid them farewell. Follow me."

With much grumbling and moaning the men finally did as they were told. Their reward was the sight of the ice sculptures.

How beautiful they were. Each of the trapped men captured for all eternity in a moment of rugged, albeit, frozen handsomeness. None of these men would ever age, hunger, or cry, ever again.

The humble man touched each sculpture and openly wept, greeting each by name. His tears fell on the sculptures and caused them to melt, little by little. His followers did the same. Soon the tears flowed so freely that each sculpture broke apart to reveal their living friends within.

The humble man's actions reunited all of them in the most beautiful moment. They shared hugs and words of regret. They were no longer as rugged, or as handsome as they had been whilst enclosed in ice, but they wept true tears of joy that they lived. They could now go home to their beloved family and friends.

The Old Man bellowed so loudly that all could hear him. "Humble man, you are blessed by a natural inclination to fortune and good sense. Your heart is kind. Take one stone–a magical Sphene–back to your village. You are worthy. It will make your harvest plentiful forever more."

The humble man wept, glad that he had not succumbed to greed's desire and had received a reward for his earnestness. He paused for a moment unsure how to proceed. Which stone was a Sphene? His fingers trailed the masses of crystals and alighted on one. It was plain compared to the rest, a clump of layered plates and flattened wedge-shaped crystals. But when he placed it in his hands it glowed in a dazzling array of colours.

He cried, his friends cried too, and they hugged each other. They started to move back towards the mouth of the cave.

The snow snake hissed. "How dare you, Old Man? I thought you were joking! That Sphene is our treasure. My treasure! Stop this immediately, or I will kill them all."

Inside the cave, there was a rustling noise as a billion tiny snow snakes appeared, hissing in fury, they slithered menacingly towards the men. The men clutched their hearts in fear, their eyes wide with panic.

The Old Man didn't reply. Not one word slipped from his lips. Instead, he blew from his mouth, and continued to blow. It blew the tiny snakes back, tumbling and rolling into snowballs whence they had come. The wind picked up as a flurry of snow began to trickle from the Snow Snake's body. The men ran, the Snow Snake started to break apart, as small pieces of the entrance of the cave crashed pummelled by the wind.

"Hurry!" shouted the Old Man. "If you don't run, the Snow Snake's broken cave body will crush you."

The men ran as fast as they could. Just as they exited the mouth of the cave the roof of the snow snake cave began to crumble further.

The Snow Snake's mouth blew apart in a final raging hiss before it crushed back together, closing the entrance to the cave forever more.

The men collapsed to the ground, safe but breathing heavily.

Once the humble man had recovered his breath he spoke. "Why did you protect and save us, mere strangers to you, above your companion the snow snake?"

The Old Man of Snow lifted his hand and cupped the area around where his heart would have rested. "There is no room for a greedy heart. It is lonely to live alone but it better to live alone than to blight the gift of true magic with greed."

My Heart Is A Cave

My heart is a cave.
Hidden dark and mysterious,
Stalactites and icy caverns,
Rock pools and hiding places.

―――

No one visits anymore. I'm alone.
The ice is melting, and the stars seem so far away.
I long for light, life and laughter to discover me again.
I wait.

―――

While I wait ice drips in darling drops,
Drip, dripping.
The moon is high,
An orb of brilliant light, it grins at me.

―――

I remember my past, days ago,
Children, a husband, lovers - even.
So, I wait for someone to come,
For a torch to shine.

―――

It comforts me that the moon is full.
Abundant.
Soon I will be reunited with you.
I imagine you smiling down on the cave.

Annette opens the attic door searching for a keepsake box. It is in the furthest corner behind many old ornaments, suitcases and forgotten things. Her hands tremble as she picks it up. She takes it down into the living room and opens the lid a smidgen but closes it abruptly. Her hands tremble with anticipation. She stops, realising that this is not the right place to open the box. Instead, she finds a carrier bag and pops the box into the bottom of the roomy bag. Her destination isn't far away. She is glad it is a weekday morning; it will be quiet in the botanical garden's glasshouses.

The lady in the entry booth is busy with other visitors and barely looks up as she enters; Annette is glad not to stop to talk. Driven by a need to open the letter she rushes ahead, only slowing her pace when she arrives at the glasshouse entrance. Now, she takes her time pausing with intention, taking in the many flowers that Harold would have loved. In the furthest tropical glasshouse, she searches for a seat but there are none, only the warm radiators to lean against. Her eyes search to see if anyone is coming and when she is sure it is quiet, she reaches in her bag and pulls out the box and then the letter. The correspondence is pale blue, folded by her guilt, its size diminished until it's only a tiny rectangle of heartfelt wishes. Its once crisp, frayed edges make her gasp.

She shakes her head; her eyes heavy with sorrow. With tender care she opens the wounded letter, fearful that it may turn to dust in her hands. As she reads it, she recognises Harold's beautiful copperplate writing and becomes overcome with an overwhelming rush of emotion. Her tears spill on the paper, watering the dormant buds of the poignant words sealed within. The paper crumbles, fragments falling to the fertile ground where a flower, or plant might grow. Her eyes widen in surprise as the dust of the letter mingles with the soil of future beauties. There is a fizzing sound, and the soil bounces about as if it is delighted to receive this magical fertiliser.

Annette stares at the spot transfixed, with wild eyes overcome by the enchanting moment she has witnessed, expecting a shoot to burst from of the soil she is disappointed when the earth surrenders to the quiet and remains still. But she feels a promise in the air and knows it will come.

Soon, her attention returns to the box. It is no longer plain, or unadorned. Instead, a rainbow graces the lid of the box. How did that happen, she wonders? She leaves it amongst the floral beauties of the greenhouse. It pleases her that perhaps someone might pick up such a pretty box; she has no need for it anymore. With, a fond backward glance she exits the greenhouses. On her way, she passes by a few strangers who greet her with warm smiles. There are no strangers here; nature only has friends.

She sits on the bench by the weeping willow tree and almost immediately a robin comes to join her. His friend the dragonfly arrives too. The three of them spend awhile together in a sweet silence which is breathtaking in its kindness. The robin moves closer to her and then hops under her feet to explore the ground beneath the bench. The dragonfly hovers above her for a moment as if saying goodbye. Her eyes close and she drifts off to sleep. When she awakes, she finds a massive ginger tom cat snoozing by her side. It is the biggest cat she has ever seen. They rest together for a while enjoying each other's tranquil company.

Mr. Sagittarius

I know I am dying so I bid all my loves and especially my dearest orchid a final farewell. I pray I will surrender my soul to a place that will be as sweet as this hot house garden. I have a bequest in my pocket. It includes a generous sum of money for a park bench in honour of this magnificent garden. I will ask for you to engrave a few simple words upon my bench when I pass to the garden of death.

It must say:

Mr. Sagittarius Died This Day in This Snow Drop Garden

Forgive me – I am ninety-two,
I forgot all but two of my lovers' names,
My first and my last.
But I remember my orchid.
Love is a garden.
Oh, so divine.

Every day my old limbs pay a visit to the Botanic Garden in Cambridge. I hate routine, but my aching joints oblige when my lonely soul seeks feminine company. It is winter and in this season of chills, snow and ice my favourite haunt is the glasshouses. In which my ancient heart warms, and I reminisce about...

LOVE

My eyes begin a familiar journey. First alighting on one of many beauties, my first love! The bird of paradise flower which I stumbled across in Papua New Guinea when I was an innocent. I was an adventurer, then. But, once awakened by the attentions of Ruth I became a Casanova! I fell in love, or perhaps in lust with Ruth–a dark-skinned beauty. I still remember the curve of her youthful skin and the way she used to gyrate her hips to entice me to join her in bed.

I linger in silent contemplation remembering Ruth and our amorous nights. Oh, what regrets followed the sudden demise of our fiery liaison. The never-ending jealousies were a sign of my Sagittarius failings, and may I dare say it?

My inability to commit.

Here I go again. Even at my advanced age my old knees fight the urge to rest and move on... longing to see... my next conquest...

There she is! Oh sigh. What a divine creature. Twirling on tiptoe, my ballerina flower. Yes, how you could dance, pirouetting on pointe. I remember you in Swan Lake. How perfect you were, your tutu twirling around as your hair remained still. Such a picture of perfection with that tight bun. How I relished swiftly untwirling your hair and removing all your silken lovelies the very same night. And dare I say it? There was an encore! But even you could not keep my attention for long. Not when there was such a fire in my belly.

There she is! Wicked creature, I blame this red glory for breaking us up.

She rose up to demand my attention like a pompon ablaze, sharp-witted with outrageous spikes of character. Oh, how this strange flower reminds me of her. She had bright red hair, and such a quirky personality. I was hooked and yet, I regret, her true name escapes me, so I nickname you Calliandra. My mind is not as sharp as it used to be. Please forgive me, my beautiful red bonnet.

If by any chance we ever meet again, I would rest my head on your shoulder. I'd begin by stroking your hair to get close to you. I'd caress you until intoxicated by your scent. I would trace tiny trails of tender kisses down your perfect body. Sigh, the memory of this is almost too much for me. I feel giddy. Let me rest for a moment in a quiet corner. Or, I fear that some well-meaning but overzealous first aider will attach that defibrillator to me! Please don't bother. It's not needed.

I should have known you wouldn't let me rest, you selfish wench!

Narcissus, my daffodil.

You command attention and I obey. Your beauty is cunning and without compare and yet I sense there is something lacking.

You are too selfish.

You cannot love.

My orchid....

I should have visited you first. Please forgive me my dearest sweetheart. You were the most exquisite of them all. My last, my first true love, an oriental flower, slender, graceful, full of charm, but, oh so fragile. I should have known. Oh, how I miss you. Now I am a ghost and lost without you. I settle for you, forgetting all others. Now I, this ghost of regret, understands the true nature of love. And now you pay me back for my thoughtlessness–your cruel ghost avoids me.

How could you be so wicked?

Perhaps you never died.

True beauty never does.

Annette wakes up, the ginger tom cat has disappeared. She turns to look at the water flowing in the pond behind the Golden Weeping Willow tree but the shock of seeing a newly engraved inscription on the park bench captures her full attention.

It says:

> *For Harold, and his brother William who so loved the garden, the hothouses, and the magical creatures of this botanical kingdom.*

> *We remember Mr. Sagittarius and his dear sweet orchid.*
> *Love is a garden.*
> *Oh, so divine.*

Annette touches the inscription with her fingertips, feeling each word in her heart she weeps, treasuring her tears.

Leaving behind the garden, her steps become lighter and more certain. She smiles.

Shortly after her departure two youngsters arrive in the glasshouses, the youngest of which picks up the box.

"Look," Lucy cries.

"What's that?" asks her brother.

"Oh, isn't this so unusual?" says Lucy as she stares at the Sagittarius centaur image on the side of the box. The lid is rainbow coloured. Inside, she discovers two notes written on blue paper. She unfolds the first.

Sagittarius
Are fun loving and childlike,
And adventurous,
Humorous, Intuitive,
Intelligent optimists.

The second note says:

Keep me safe and place your happy most treasured thoughts and wishes here, in sketches, words and pictures.

Mr. Sagittarius

While the siblings are engrossed reading Mr Sagittarius's messages the stem of a magnificent tropical flower emerges from the soil. It is in full bloom by the time Lucy has finished reading the two notes.

"Look at that!" she exclaims, touching the flower's pretty petals.

"I swear that flower wasn't there a moment ago. This is strange Lucy, perhaps you shouldn't take that box, maybe it belongs to someone, like an evil wizard or something."

Lucy punches her brother in the arm and says, "Don't be an idiot Daniel. Haven't you heard of the legend of Mr. Sagittarius? There's a park bench by the golden willow tree which is named after him and his twin brother William. Mr. Sagittarius is mysterious and magical in a good way. The natural world loves him. This will bring us luck."

"Wow! Shall we buy a lottery ticket?"

"Daniel! Aren't you paying attention? Mr. Sagittarius will bring magic into our lives, but don't you know anything? Money and the natural world don't mix. Magic is far more amazing than any amount of money. Money can't buy magic! Magic is Magic."

The End

Reviews mean so much to authors. If you enjoyed this book, I would be so very grateful if you would consider leaving a review. Thank you in anticipation.

Acknowledgements

A big thank you to Colleen Chesebro for encouraging me to write poetry with her weekly poetry challenges. Also, I'd like to extend a thank you to Charli Mills at Carrot Ranch Literary Community for introducing me to flash fiction and to author Diana Peach and Rachael Ritchey for their writing prompts.

https://colleenchesebro.com/
https://carrotranch.com/
https://mythsofthemirror.com/
https://blogbattlers.wordpress.com/

Also, the multi-talented Rachael Ritchey did a wonderful job creating the fantastic cover for Mr. Sagittarius.

About the Author

M J Mallon was born in Lion city Singapore, a passionate Scorpio with the Chinese Zodiac sign of a lucky rabbit. She spent her early childhood in Hong Kong. During her teen years, she returned to her father's childhood home, Edinburgh where she spent many happy years, entertained and enthralled by her parents' vivid stories of living and working abroad. Perhaps it was during these formative years that her love of storytelling began bolstered by these vivid raconteurs. She counts herself lucky to have travelled to many far-flung destinations and this early wanderlust has fuelled her present desire to emigrate abroad. Until that wondrous moment, it's rumoured that she lives somewhere in the UK, with her six-foot hunk of a rock god husband. Her two enchanting daughters have flown the nest but often return with a cheery smile.

Her motto is to always do what you love, stay true to your heart's desires, and inspire others to do so too, even it if appears that the odds are stacked against you like black hearted shadows.

MJ's favourite genres to write are YA fantasy, paranormal, ghost and horror stories, and various forms of poetry and flash fiction, because life should be sprinkled with a liberal dash of extraordinarily imaginative magic!

She celebrates bookish wonders, the spiritual realm and all things magical, mystical and mysterious at her blog home:

https://mjmallon.com/

Also By M J Mallon

❧

Next Chapter Publishing
YA Fantasy series, The Curse of Time
For details of publications please visit:
https://www.nextchapter.pub/authors/mj-mallon

❧

Kyrosmagica Publishing
The Hedge Witch And The Musical Poet
https://books2read.com/u/mv1OeV
Anthology - This Is Lockdown
http://mybook.to/Thisislockdown
Poetry during Lockdown - Lockdown Innit
http://mybook.to/Lockdowninnit

❧

Short Stories in Anthologies:
Wings & Fire edited by Dan Alatorre
https://www.amazon.co.uk/dp/B08KJ5SQND
Spellbound edited by Dan Alatorre
https://www.amazon.co.uk/gp/product/B08DM83XKR/
Nightmareland edited by Dan Alatorre –
https://www.amazon.co.uk/gp/product/1702784886/

For all my publications and contributions to anthologies please refer to my author blog: https://mjmallon.com/
Amazon author page: https://www.amazon.co.uk/M-J-Mallon/e/B074CGNK4L/

www.ingramcontent.com/pod-product-compliance
Lightning Source LLC
Chambersburg PA
CBHW041025170626
46815CB00001B/12